# UP NEXT >>>

:02  *SPORTS ZONE SPECIAL REPORT*

:04  **FEATURE PRESENTATION:**

# SKATEBOARD SONAR

## FOLLOWED BY:

:50  **SPORTS ZONE POSTGAME RECAP**

:51  **SPORTS ZONE POSTGAME EXTRA**

:52  **SI KIDS INFO CENTER**

**XT**
BOARDING

## BLIND SKATER COMPETES FOR STREET COURSE TITLE!

# MATTHEW LYONS

**STATS:**
NICKNAME: MATTY
AGE: 13
EVENT: STREET

**BIO:** Matty is blind, but you wouldn't know it by watching him skate — he has become a top-notch street course skater despite his disability. Matty has also developed a reputation as a local hero for his difficult grabs, stellar tricks, and positive attitude. Matty is almost always seen with his skateboard, and his best buddy, Ty, nearby.

UP NEXT: SKATEBOARD SONAR

# TYSON TAGGART

**NICKNAME: TY**
**AGE: 13  EVENT: HALFPIPE**

**BIO:** Ty is a hot-head who reigns supreme on the halfpipe. He skates hard and loves to put on a good show. Ty has been best friends with Matty Lyons since kindergarten.

## CLINTON WASHBURN

**NICKNAME: CLINT  AGE: 13  EVENT: HALFPIPE**
**BIO:** Clint's a talented boarder who's trouble on — and off — the halfpipe. His best buddy is the big bully, Bing Hawtin.

**WASHBURN**

## BINGLEY HAWTIN

**NICKNAME: BING  AGE: 14  EVENT: STREET**
**BIO:** The only thing Bing likes to do more than pick on puny skaters is beat them senseless on the street course.

**HAWTIN**

## JILLIAN SPEARS

**NICKNAME: JILLY  AGE: 17  JOB: PARK OWNER**
**BIO:** Jilly's a true patron of the skating art. A talented skater herself, Jilly's park will host the All-City Skating Competition.

**SPEARS**

**Sports Illustrated KID$**

*PRESENTS*

# SKATEBOARD SONAR

*A PRODUCTION OF*

**STONE ARCH BOOKS**
a capstone imprint

*written by* Eric Stevens
*illustrated by* Gerardo Sandoval
*colored by* Benny Fuentes

*designed and directed by* Bob Lentz
*edited by* Sean Tulien
*creative direction by* Heather Kindseth
*editorial direction by* Michael Dahl

Sports Illustrated Kids *Skateboard Sonar* is published by Stone Arch Books,
151 Good Counsel Drive, P.O. Box 669, Mankato, Minnesota 56002.
www.capstonepub.com

Summary: Matty Lyons can do all the coolest tricks. His moves are even more
impressive since he's blind. But not everyone is a fan of the talented grinder.
During the state's biggest skating competition, former champion Bing Hawtin
mocks Matty, saying that a blind kid has no chance to win. But Matty knows
something Bing doesn't . . . seeing isn't everything.

Library of Congress Cataloging-in-Publication Data
Stevens, Eric.
 Skateboard sonar / written by Eric Stevens ; illustrated by Gerardo
Sandoval, illustrated by Benny Fuentes.
  p. cm. -- (Sports Illustrated Kids graphic novels)
 ISBN 978-1-4342-1910-7 (library binding) -- ISBN 978-1-4342-2295-4
(pbk.) 1. Graphic novels. [1. Graphic novels. 2. Skateboarding--Fiction. 3.
Blind--Fiction. 4. People with disabilities--Fiction.]
I. Sandoval, Gerardo, ill. II. Fuentes, Benny, ill. III. Title.
 PZ7.7.S79Sk 2010
 741.5973--dc22                          2009037870

Printed in the United States of America in Stevens Point, Wisconsin.
102010    005977R

Matthew Lyons always looks forward to Fridays.

Because every Friday after school, Matt and his friend Ty skateboard until dark.

Ready to roll, Matt?

Yep! Just let me get my board!

Listen up, students. School is now in session!

Haha, yeah! Watch and learn!

WHIRRRR

Good afternoon, Matt.

Hello there, Ty.

Hey, Mrs. Greentree!

Most Fridays, Matt and Ty just skate around their neighborhood.

But today is no ordinary Friday.

Sounds like a full house.

Yep. We better go sign up!

Watch your mouth, jerk!

You gonna make me?

Don't bother, Ty. You'll prove them wrong in the halfpipe.

Right.

And you'll embarrass *him* on the street course.

No way. I've won the street contest at six other skateparks this year.

WOOOOSH!!

No way!

Nice moves, Matty.

I knew it was there the whole time.

Echolocation. It's how bats get around in the dark.

See, the wheels on a skateboard make a sound.

So you can tell when something is in your way?

But that trashcan could still have hurt Matty!

I'm Matty. And this is Ty.

Nice to meet you.

What's this? You making nice with this loser, Clint?

You want to be his seeing-eye dog or something?

That's it. Now I'm mad.

Wait, Ty —

Soon, Ty and Clint entered the halfpipe...

Clint Washburn earns an 8.9!

WHOOSH

That's an 8.8 for Ty Taggart!

KRRRRRR

...and Matty skated against Bing on the street course.

That's a 9.1 for Bing Hawtin!

KLANK!

And Matty Lyons gets a 9.0!

31

Later...

All-City Skateboarding Competition Finalists

Did we make the finals?

Let's push through so I can get a look at the standings.

Lead the way.

Pardon us. Coming through.

Excuse me.

Yes! I'm in the halfpipe finals!

I saw that coming.

What about me?

Skateboard Competition Finalists

**Pipeline Course**
- J. Break
- Ty
- Clint

**Street C...**
- B. Fuente...
- Carbon...
- Matt
- Bing

Hmm . . . I don't see you here.

What?!

Just kidding, buddy. You're in the finals.

Whew. You had me for a second.

I'm starving. Let's get some grub.

Cool. Jilly's serving free burgers out back!

square"? A blind kid in the contest? Yeah, right.

He did great on the street course, Bing.

I wasn't watching.

Then again, I guess he wasn't, either!

Hahaha!

Man, that guy is a real bully.

At least he'll be gone once the competition is over.

Hey there, boys!

Hi, Jilly! Thanks for volunteering your skatepark for the competition.

Yeah! It's been great so far.

I'm not so sure about that, Matty.

What do you mean?

Those two bullies are going around picking on everyone.

Yeah, we met them.

Should I kick them out of the competition?

Yeah! For unsportsmanlike conduct!

All-City Skateboarding Competition Finals

The halfpipe finals are down to two skaters . . .

. . . Ty Taggart and Clint Washburn!

Ready for this, pal?

Pfft. This pipe is mine.

WOOOSH

LYONS

# BLIND SKATER BEATS BULLY BOARDER ON THE STREET COURSE!

**STORY:** Six-time street course champion, Bing Hawtin, finally met his match earlier today when blind skater, Matthew Lyons, took home the All-City trophy. Matty earned many new fans in his two routines for his creativity and technical skill. When asked how he felt about being a blind skater, Matt was quoted as saying that "seeing isn't everything."

## Sports Illustrated KIDS

**UP NEXT: SI KIDS INFO CENTER**

POWERED BY **STONE ARCH**

BLZ vs BKS
**3·1**
TGR vs ROR
**33·32***
EAG vs BAN
**14·7**
SPA vs WLD*
**4·3**
BAN vs ROR
**21·15**
ROR vs LIG
**4·3**
BLZ vs BKS

# SZ POSTGAME EXTRA
WHERE **YOU** ANALYZE THE GAME!

Skateboarding fans got a real treat today when Matty one-upped runner-up, Bing Hawtin, on the street course. Let's go into the stands and ask some fans for their opinions on the day's events ...

## DISCUSSION QUESTION 1

Matty is blind, but he didn't let his disability prevent him from skateboarding. If you were blind, how would your life be different? How would it be the same?

## DISCUSSION QUESTION 2

Ty Taggart had some trouble managing his anger. What do you do when you get angry? Can anger ever be a good thing? Why or why not?

## WRITING PROMPT 1

Bing the bully is out to get Matt and Ty. Have you ever had to deal with a bully? What happened? Write about your bully experience.

## WRITING PROMPT 2

Matty and Ty win the street course and halfpipe competitions, respectively. Have you ever competed for something? What happened? Write about it.

(AIR)—if you grab air, you are riding with all four skateboard wheels off the ground

(KON-duhkt)—behavior

(ek-oh-loh-KAY-shuhn)—the method of locating something by determining the time for an echo to return to its source, like with radar or sonar

(GRAB)—if you perform a grab, you hold on to your skateboard and strike a pose in midair

(GRINDE)—if you do a grind, you skate with one or both axles of your board on a curb, railing, or other surface

(HAF-pipe)—a U-shaped ramp of any size, usually with a flat section in the middle, that is used for skateboarding

(SY-tid)—if you are sighted, then you are able to see. Sighted is the opposite of blind.

(uhn-SPORTS-muhn-like)—not displaying the behavior of a good sport, or to play dirty

# CREATORS

### ERIC STEVENS › Author

Eric Stevens lives in St. Paul, Minnesota. He is studying to become a middle-school English teacher. His favorite things include pizza, video games, watching cooking shows on TV, riding his bike, and trying new restaurants. Some of his least favorite things include olives and shoveling snow.

### GERARDO SANDOVAL › Illustrator

Gerardo Sandoval is a professional comic book illustrator from Mexico. He has worked on many well-known comics including the Tomb Raider books from Top Cow Productions. He has also worked on designs for posters and card sets.

### BENNY FUENTES › Colorist

Benny Fuentes lives in Villahermosa, Tabasco in Mexico, where it's just as hot as the sauce is. He studied graphic design in college, but now he works as a full-time colorist in the comic book industry for companies like Marvel, DC Comics, and Top Cow Productions. He shares his home with two crazy cats, Chelo and Kitty, who act like they own the place.

# WAIT!